For Emma, Theo, Natasha, Ben, and Gloria
—M. R.

For Simon and Diane
—S. B.

Henry Holt and Company, LLC
PUBLISHERS SINCE 1866
175 Fifth Avenue
New York, New York 10010
www.HenryHoltKids.com

Library of Congress Cataloging-in-Publication Data
Rosoff, Meg. Wild boars cook / Meg Rosoff and Sophie Blackall.—1st ed.
p.   cm.
Summary: Besides being naughty, greedy, stinky, and rude, wild boars Boris, Morris, Horace, and Doris
are also very hungry and luckily Doris finds the perfect recipe for them to make.
ISBN-13: 978-0-8050-7523-6 / ISBN-10: 0-8050-7523-2
[1. Wild boar—Fiction. 2. Behavior—Fiction. 3. Cookery—Fiction. 4. Humorous stories.] I. Blackall, Sophie, ill. II. Title.
PZ7.R719563Wil 2008   [E]—dc22   2007040899

First Edition—2008 / Designed by Patrick Collins / Hand lettering by Sophie Blackall
The artist used Chinese ink and watercolor on hot-press paper to create the illustrations for this book.
Printed in China on acid-free paper. ∞

1 3 5 7 9 10 8 6 4 2

WILD BOARS COOK

MEG ROSOFF AND SOPHIE BLACKALL

Henry Holt and Company ✦ New York

This is Boris.

This is Morris.

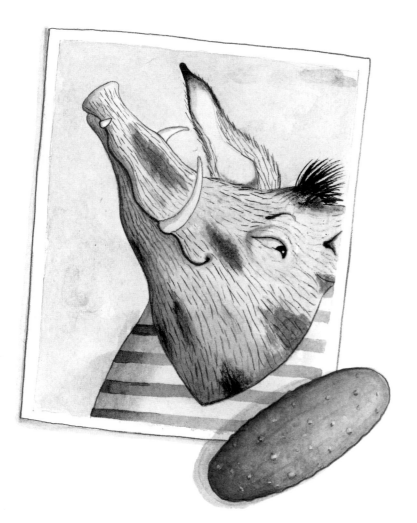

This is Horace.

This is Doris.
They are wild boars.

They are bossy

and selfish

and stinky

and HUNGRY.

Boris is so hungry he could eat

35 hot dogs

and a bushel of bonbons.

CRUNCH CRUNCH CRUNCH

Bad Boris.

Morris is so hungry he could eat
a pineapple upside-down cake,
ten pickles, and a boot.

MUNCH MUNCH MUNCH

Naughty Morris.

Horace is so hungry he could eat
a pizza as big as the moon.

YUM YUM YUM

Horrid Horace.

YUM
YUM
YUM

Doris is so hungry she is eating

a cookbook.

But wait!
Doris has found a delicious recipe.
A recipe for the biggest,
messiest, stickiest,
gooiest, chewiest,
most delicious pudding
in the whole wide world.

Watch out, everybody.
Wild boars are making
a Massive Pudding!

First they measure out
the ingredients.

"Ten cups of sugar!"
shouts Morris.

"Five hundred
chocolate-covered chocolates!"
roars Boris.

"A gross of donuts,"
squeals Horace.

"And lots and lots of broccoli!"
shrieks Doris.

Everybody stops and stares.
Broccoli?
In a Massive Pudding?

"Sorry," said Doris.

(Almost) all the ingredients went
into a massive pudding bowl.

"It's too dry," sobbed Boris.

"It's too small," wailed Morris.

"I'm hungry," howled Horace.

So Doris added one and a half puddles,

a bucket of squishy butter,

26 bananas,

and a squid.

Then started to whisk briskly.

All the boars joined in.

WHISK WHISK WHISK!

STIR STIR STIR!

COOK COOK COOK!

And out came the most beautiful
Massive Pudding in the whole wide world.

Now, do you think
Boris and Morris and Horace and Doris
sat with their hands folded
and their napkins in their laps?
Did they pass the biggest piece
to the wild boar on their left?
Did they say thank you
and chew with their mouths closed?

Of course not!

They gulped and grabbed
and smashed and snatched
and pushed and prodded
and choked and chewed....
And they ate that Massive Pudding
in ten seconds flat.

"Delightful," moaned Boris.

"Delicious," groaned Morris.

"Divine," burped Horace.

"It was my idea," said Doris.

And they all lived happily ever after
for five whole minutes.

Until . . .

"I'm still hungry,"
cried Boris.

"I'm still starving,"
wept Morris.

"Everyone got more than me," howled Horace.

"Never mind," said Doris.

"I think I've found another recipe."

MASSIVE COOKIE
(makes one)

$\frac{1}{2}$ cup butter

1 cup sugar

1 egg

$\frac{1}{2}$ teaspoon vanilla

1 cup flour

$\frac{1}{2}$ teaspoon salt

$\frac{1}{2}$ teaspoon baking soda

$\frac{1}{2}$ cup chocolate chips

$\frac{1}{2}$ cup gumdrops

$\frac{1}{4}$ cup M&Ms

Preheat oven to 375 degrees. Cream together butter and sugar. Add egg and vanilla. Stir in flour, salt, and baking soda. Add chocolate chips. Form into one large cookie on greased cookie sheet and decorate with gumdrops and M&Ms. Bake for about half an hour or until done. Do not attempt to make or devour the cookie without an adult present.